USBORNE CASTLE TALES

THE LITTLE DRAGON

Heather Amery
Illustrated by Stephen Cartwright

Language consultant: Betty Root
Series editor: Jenny Tyler

There is a little yellow duck to find on every page.

This is Grey Stone Castle.

This is King Leo and Queen Rose. They have two children called Prince Max and Princess Alice.

Max and Alice are playing outside.

Max is a knight and Alice is a dragon. "Let's go and find a real dragon," says Max.

They go out of the castle gate.

"We're going to find a dragon," says Alice.
"There aren't any dragons," says the guard.

They walk across the bridge.

Then Max and Alice walk along the road up a hill.
"Will we find a real dragon?" says Alice.

"There's a cave," says Max.

"Dragons live in caves. I hope we find a dragon in it." "I wish King Dad was here," says Alice.

They look into the cave.

"Come out, dragon," shouts Max. He waves
his sword. "There's nothing there," says Alice.

"Look at that," says Max.

A puff of smoke and flames come out of the cave.
"Let's go home now," says Alice.

"What do you want?"

A dragon walks out. "I was asleep. You woke me up," he says. He yawns and shows his teeth.

"You don't scare me."

"I am a princess," says Alice. "You are only a small dragon. So don't be so cross and grumpy."

"Sorry," says the dragon.

He bows his head. "I'm so hungry. Every time I ask anyone for food, they run away," he says.

"Come with us," says Max.

They walk down the hill. The dragon runs after them. "Wait for me," he says.

Max and Alice go back to the castle.

The King comes out. "What's that?" he says.
Old Gus, a servant, hides behind the door.

"It's a very hungry dragon."

"Bring a very large dragon breakfast, please,"
says the King to Old Gus.

"Here comes your food," says Max.

Old Gus brings a huge plate of food. He puts it on the ground. "Thank you," says the dragon.

"May we keep him, please?" says Alice.

"Yes," says the King. "He can have three meals a day and light the castle fires for us."

First published in 1996 by Usborne Publishing Ltd, 83-85 Saffron Hill, London EC1N 8RT, England. Copyright © Usborne Publishing Ltd.
The name Usborne and the device ♔ are Trade Marks of Usborne Publishing Ltd. All rights reserved. No part of this publication may be reproduced, stored in a retrieval system, or transmitted in any form or by any means, electronic, mechanical, photocopy, recording or otherwise, without prior permission of the publisher. UE First published in America in August 1996. Printed in Italy.

1549